This book belongs to

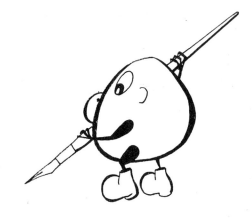

© 1976 Michael Cooper
First published in Great Britain in 1976 by
CRESSRELLES PUBLISHING COMPANY LIMITED
Kestrels House, Peppard Common, Oxfordshire

ISBN 0 85956 020 1 case-bound edition
     0 85956 021 X card-cover edition

Printed in Great Britain by Burgess & Son (Abingdon) Ltd

THE PEBBLES NIGHT ADVENTURE

by Michael Cooper

It was a hot and sunny day on the beach. Children played everywhere. They swam and paddled in the sea all day.

One little boy, called Julian, played in the sand. He had spent all afternoon making a sandcastle. He patted the sand down with care and put a flag on the top.

He had really enjoyed his day on the beach. But there was something on the sand which he had not seen.

Among some ordinary pebbles by his sandcastle were two very odd ones.

Suddenly there was a shout from the promenade above. It was Julian's father calling him to come to the car. It was getting late and time to go home.

Julian was picking up his bucket and spade when he noticed the two odd pebbles.

He picked them up and put them in his pocket, where he already had a seashell.
"I'll put these in my collection," he said to himself.

Then he went home in the car. He was very tired and soon fell asleep on the backseat.

His mummy and daddy put him
to bed as soon as they got home.

His clothes were left on
a chair in the corner.
Everything was very quiet.

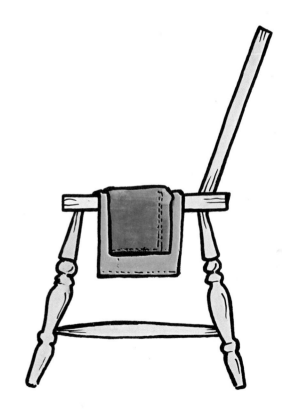

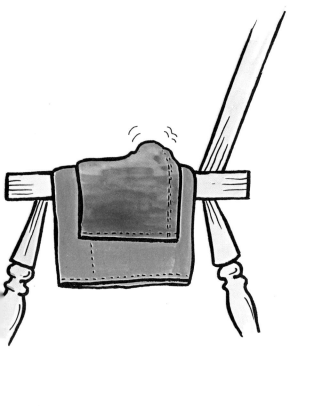

In the early hours of the morning, when only the sun was up, very strange things began to happen. Something was moving in the pocket of Julian's shorts.

First a little arm appeared, then a little red shoe —and two more arms.

Out climbed the two little pebbles
which Julian had put in his pocket.

There was Penny Pebble, who was a little worried about where she was. The last thing she remembered was going to sleep on the beach.

The other pebble, who was called Peter, was not worried at all. He loved an adventure.

Peter Pebble helped Penny down
from the chair

and led the way on tiptoe
across the bedroom floor.

In the middle of the room was
a big soft orange hill which
they climbed up.
Peter helped Penny up and up
to see what was at the top.

There they had a big surprise.
"Look, it's a boy," said Peter.
"The boy from the beach."
"Ssh, we must not wake him,"
whispered Penny.

"Let's go and explore then," Peter whispered back. He climbed down and made a slide for Penny. Down she came Wzzzz-z.

Crash! Bang! She landed on Peter,
knocking him into a big pile of
coloured bricks.

Behind the bricks Penny found a big ball to play with.

Peter was soon driving round in Julian's toy bulldozer. Suddenly he bumped into something large and soft and hairy.

It was a big furry animal,
which seemed to be asleep.

Peter climbed up the
big animal's arm and
shouted in its ear,
but he could not wake it.

"Come back Peter. Please come back," Penny shouted.
"I am scared. It might wake up and eat us."

Peter climbed quickly down to look after Penny

"It won't eat us, it's fast asleep," he said.

"I'm sleepy too," said Penny as they crept past some other toys. "We should go home now." Peter pointed to a window and told Penny how they could climb up the curtains onto the window ledge.

They were soon standing outside on the window ledge. Peter reached out and got hold of one of the huge plants there.

"We can use this as a ladder," he said. "I'll go first and see that it's safe. It's alright," he shouted when he had climbed a little way. "Come on, I'll race you."

Peter was easily the first one to reach the ground.

They ran through the garden under the flowers.

"I must have a flower," said Penny.

And she stopped to pick one,

while Peter asked a mouse
the way to the beach.
"Under the gate, down the
hill and you can't miss it,"
said the mouse.

So Peter and Penny crept out under the front gate.

Down the hill,

past the milkman who was just starting work.

Down they raced to the sea front
and to the pile of rocks which they
use as their own special steps to
the beach.

Peter jumped down the last few rocks, but Penny was very careful to look after her flower.

They were soon asleep on the sand with Penny
still holding her flower as the sun rose above the sea.